AuthorHouse™ LLC
1663 Liberty Drive
Bloomington, IN 47403
www.authorhouse.com
Phone: 1-800-839-8640

Published by AuthorHouse 09/04/2014

ISBN: 978-1-4969-3751-3 (sc)
ISBN: 978-1-4969-3752-0 (e)

Library of Congress Control Number: 2014915919

Any people depicted in stock imagery provided by Thinkstock are models,
and such images are being used for illustrative purposes only.
Certain stock imagery © Thinkstock.

This book is printed on acid-free paper.

authorHOUSE®

ABOUT THE AUTHOR

Sandra grew up in Putnam, Connecticut where she was a student in the class of Gertrude Chandler Warner, author of the Boxcar Children series. The first book in the series was published when Sandra was in Miss Warner's first grade class in 1942. Miss Warner became her mentor, first as teacher then as author. Sandra became a teacher before trying her hand at publishing. She says, "After keeping my promise to myself to become a teacher, and teaching for 55 years, I decided I should keep my second promise – to become a published author, just like my mentor." Miss Warner took time to pique the interest of children. We experienced the learning. Mrs. Ames is continuing her teaching career and now taking time to write children's stories. She lives in Putnam, Connecticut where she enjoys the rural life of her childhood. She desires to share the simple things of life with her reading audience. "Nature has a way of bringing things together and teaching us lessons," she says. This book features events in our history and makes history interesting for children.

ABOUT THE ILLUSTRATOR

Rebecca Pempek, age 15, lives in Connecticut. She is an honors student at Pomfret School. She started making sketches for <u>Two Frogs on a Bike</u> at age 12. Rebecca has exhibited and sold her art work. She spent two weeks in the summer of 2013 at an intensive art program, L'Atelier au Chateau, in Mussy sur Seine, France. She continues to pursue her art career at Pomfret as she anticipates the college selection process.

ACKNOWLEDGEMENTS

I would like to thank my mentor, Gertrude Chandler Warner posthumously, for introducing me to the world of learning. Her teaching awakened my imagination and quest for knowledge. She encouraged creativity and the love of learning.

A special thank you to my family. I am fortunate that my Dad and Mom emphasized education and provided a positive learning environment at home. Thanks also to sisters Louise and Carol, husband Dave, daughters Deborah and Susan, for encouraging and supporting me along the way in this endeavor.

Another note of thanks to the little antique shop by the side of the road in Hanover, Virginia for its sign - TWO FROGS ON A BIKE ANTIQUE SHOP. This sign stirred my imagination and desire to write this book.

Thanks also to my grand niece, Rebecca Pempek, for her willingness to share her outstanding talent in illustrating this book.

Finally, thank you to Susan Salesses, friend and colleague, who edited the book.

Two Frogs on a Bike

Written by

Sandra Ames

Illustrated by

Rebecca Pempek

Very early one morning there was a strange noise; a squeak coming from the dark corner of the shed. A small, green frog suddenly woke up when he heard the noise. His name was Freddy.

Freddy decided he should check out the noise and find out where it was coming from. He hopped quickly and quietly through the doorway, stopping to listen. He heard the noise again, so he continued hopping toward it.

His final hop landed him right in the middle of a big puddle.
Upon investigating, he found water slowly dripping into a swinging
pail hanging on a nail above the puddle.

9

Freddy the frog was happy because the noise was not going to harm him. He turned around and hopped out of the shed and around the corner. There he spied a rusty bike resting against the old antique shop.

Freddy got a terrific idea! Wouldn't it be fun to ride a bike around the countryside? He would be able to see many more sights. He could travel much faster and hopefully not get as tired as if he had hopped. But he had no bike!

Freddy thought to himself, "Maybe I could borrow THIS bike. I would return it as soon as I get back." He knocked on the door of the store. He waited. No one answered. He knocked again. Same result. No answer. He could leave a note, but he saw no paper or pencil.

Freddy sat down and thought. "What should I do?" Finally he decided to leave a note in the sand. With a sharp stick he wrote in the sand near the bike, "TOOK THE BIKE. NO, BORROWED THE BIKE. WILL RETURN IT SOON," signed Freddy.

Now for that bike ride! As he climbed up on the bike seat he heard a familiar sound. "Ribbit." He turned and saw his friend Philip, also a frog.

"Would you like to come with me on my journey?" asked Freddy.

"Ribbit, ribbit," croaked Philip. "I'd love to come with you, but where are you going?"

"Probably as far as the big river," replied Freddy.

Philip quickly climbed up on the bike and away they went. Oh, what fun they had as they saw the world from the bike! The small road led them past many farms and lovely homes. They noticed many small streams and muddy ponds along the way.

Finally, they got to the BIG RIVER. The river looked like it went on forever! Freddy and Philip got off the bike and leaped toward the bank of the river. They tried to find out if they could see where the river ended.

They decided to hop back on the bike and follow the river for a while. The sun shone brightly as it glistened on the water. How warm and comfortable they felt as they pedaled their way on the path next to the river.

In a short time, they saw something in the distance that they didn't recognize. What could those things be? They pedaled a little faster. Soon they got as close as they dared.

RP

They were chatting between themselves, discussing the strange sight, when they heard "Ribbit." Who was that?

They answered "Ribbit, ribbit." From around the corner hopped a small, green frog who recognized them. Susie was one of their friends from years ago. They chatted eagerly about the fun they had in the days when they played together in the old millpond.

"How did you get HERE?" Philip questioned.

Ribbit!

"Do you remember the twins who visited each summer? Well, one day that freckled face boy stuffed me into his pocket and took me with him.

He carried me all the way to his home, up there on the hill," explained Susie.

"What did you do then?" questioned Freddy.

"I hopped away," answered Susie. "I found myself here at the river's edge. I then jumped onto some boards which led me to a dark corner on a ship. That ship was called *Discovery*."

"Oh, is that what you call those things — ships?" croaked Freddy.

"Yes, and I'll tell you a story about them," replied Susie. " I heard this story as I hid away in the corner of that small ship. A guide was speaking to the people who had come aboard. He explained that there were three ships altogether. They carried people who wanted to form a new settlement and find gold or other treasures."

"The guide said there had been twenty-one settlers on the ship called *Discovery*. That big one, the *Susan Constant*, carried seventy-one people. Fifty-two settlers crowded onto the middle sized ship named *Godspeed*."

"How crowded they must have been!" croaked Philip. "Did the men have to leap frog over each other in order to move around the ship? That would have looked funny!"

" I guess there couldn't have been enough room for even a frog," added Philip.

"These ships all left England in December of 1606. Finally, after a dangerous four and a half month voyage, they arrived here in April of 1607. We now call this place Jamestown."

"Why are the ships brightly colored?" questioned Freddy.

"The guide said the ships were painted that way so they could keep track of each other on the vast ocean," explained Susie.

Freddy's eyes were opened wide as he croaked in disbelief, "All the way across the ocean?"

"Yes," replied Susie, "and those settlers were very brave."

"Did they bring frogs like us with them?" chimed Philip.

Susie said that she didn't know about that and then she continued.
"Many, many people got sick on the voyage and they had a very hard
time when they got here. There was no food. It was hard to grow crops.
The water was dirty and they couldn't drink it. Many died. It was a
dark and unfriendly place with many Indians."

Philip questioned, "What are Indians? I never heard that word."

Susie answered, "I heard the guide say that there were people living on this land when the settlers got here. They called these people Indians. Some of the Indians were friendly, but many were not."

Freddy squeaked, "I'm afraid to go home now because there might be an unfriendly Indian watching and waiting for me."

"Don't worry," said Susie, "today's Indians are just like everyone else."

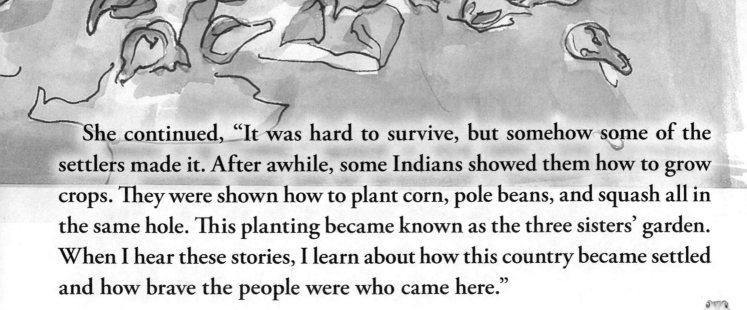

She continued, "It was hard to survive, but somehow some of the settlers made it. After awhile, some Indians showed them how to grow crops. They were shown how to plant corn, pole beans, and squash all in the same hole. This planting became known as the three sisters' garden. When I hear these stories, I learn about how this country became settled and how brave the people were who came here."

"Susie, what an interesting life you have had. Thank you for the stories. I hope we'll be able to come back again for another visit. We need to get back home and return this bike. Maybe they will let us borrow it another day," responded Freddy.

The two friends thanked Susie again, and climbed back on the bike and began pedaling as fast as they could. The sun was beginning to go down and they didn't want to lose their way.

When at last Philip and Freddy swung into the yard of the old antique shop, the sun had disappeared and dusk had settled. They parked the bike where it had been against the old shop and noticed the note was still scribbled in the sand. "I guess no one has seen our note or even realized we had borrowed the bike," croaked Freddy.

"I guess not. I'm very tired," said Philip. "See you tomorrow."

"I'm tired too. My legs are all stretched out!" yawned Freddy.

"Ribbit," sighed Philip.

"Ribbit," echoed Freddy.

Thus ended the adventure of the two frogs on a bike.

Printed in the United States
By Bookmasters